THREE
Fox
FABLES

To Sybil, Lou, and Sid

WEEKLY READER CHILDREN'S BOOK CLUB PRESENTS

THREE Aesop FOX

THE SEABURY PRESS *New York*

Copyright © 1971 by Paul Galdone. Library of Congress Catalog Card Number: 79-133061. Book designed by Paul Galdone. Printed in the United States of America. Weekly Reader Children's Book Club Edition Primary Division

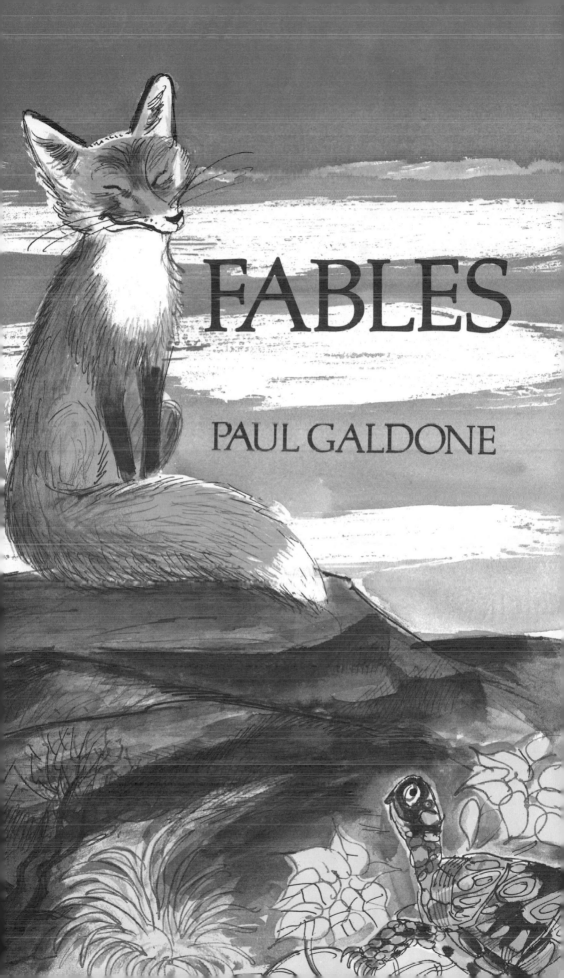

FABLES

PAUL GALDONE

The Fox
and the Grapes

ONE late summer day
the Fox was strolling
through an orchard.
Soon he came to a bunch
of ripe grapes hanging
from a lofty branch.

"Just the thing to quench my thirst," he thought.

He crouched down,
then took a run and a jump.
But he didn't go high enough.

He turned around and with
a one, two, three,
he jumped again.
But he still didn't go high enough.

Again and again the Fox tried
to reach the tempting grapes,
until at last he had to give it up.
He walked away with
his nose in the air and said:
"I am sure those grapes are sour."

IT IS EASY TO SCORN
WHAT YOU CANNOT GET

The Fox and the Stork

The Fox and the Stork were friends,
and one day he invited her to dinner.

For a joke, the Fox served soup
in very shallow dishes.
He easily lapped up the soup,
but the Stork could not get even a mouthful.
"I am sorry you do not like my soup,"
said the Fox slyly.

"Do not worry about it,"
said the Stork.
"Why don't you come and
dine with me in my marsh tomorrow?"
"I should like that," said the Fox.

He arrived at the appointed hour

only to find...

two tall, narrow vases on the grass.

The Stork easily sipped
the soup at the bottom of her vase.
But the Fox could only smell it,
and lick the side of his vase.

"I am sorry you do not like my soup,"
said the Stork.
The Fox said nothing,
and left as hungry as when he came.

TRICKSTERS CANNOT COMPLAIN
WHEN THEY IN TURN ARE TRICKED

The Fox
and the Crow

The Fox once saw a Crow fly by
with a piece of cheese in her beak.
"I want that cheese," thought the Fox.

He sat down beneath the tree and called,
"Good day, Mistress Crow!
How well you are looking!
How bright your eye!
How glossy your feathers!"
The Crow was pleased. She loved to be flattered.

"I am sure your voice is
even more beautiful than your feathers,"
cried the Fox.
"Won't you sing a song for me,
O Queen of Birds?"
The Crow was so pleased
she could hardly sit still.

She lifted her head high,
closed her eyes, and
opened her beak to sing:

CAW-W—W—!

The cheese fell to the ground,
right in front of the Fox.

"Thank you, Mistress Crow,"
he said to the unhappy bird.
"In exchange for your cheese,
I will give you a piece of advice."

NEVER TRUST A FLATTERER

And then he ate the cheese.

Aesop

Little is definitely known about the life of
AESOP. Some books say he was born in the land
of Phrygia—now central Turkey—in about 620
B.C., and brought to Greece as a slave. What is
known is that he became the most famous writ-
er of fables. Most later European fables, in-
cluding those of La Fontaine, were inspired by
Aesop's tales in which animals illustrate hu-
man vices, follies, and virtues.

PAUL GALDONE is one of the most admired and
enjoyed of contemporary American children's
book illustrators. He was drawn to the humor,
simplicity, and point of these three Aesop fables, and conceived the novel idea of linking
them in a picture book anthology.